HOW TO DRAW

By Conrad Wells
Illustrated by Ursula Albano
BATMAN created by Bob Kane

SCHOLASTIC INC.

New York   Toronto   London   Auckland   Sydney
Mexico City   New Delhi   Hong Kong   Buenos Aires

ISBN 0-439-72782-0

12 11 10 9 8 7 6 5 4 3 2 1   5 6 7 8 9/0

Printed in the U.S.A.
First printing, August 2005

IT BEGINS . . .

Prepare yourself. You are about to step into a dark world of brave heroes, vile villains, and endless adventure . . . the world of Batman. Not only will you learn how to draw the Dark Knight, you will also learn to draw his fiercest enemies.

Are you ready? You'd better be, because the fate of Gotham City is in your hands!

Just as Batman needs tools like the Batwave, the Batarang, and the Batmobile to fight crime, there are a few tools you'll need to draw. Make sure you have a pencil, paper, and an eraser ready. You might also want graph paper, a pen, markers, crayons, or even watercolor paint.

BASIC SHAPE TRAINING

The first thing you need to know is how to use the basic shapes. All of the drawings in this book are made up of a few simple — and familiar — elements: circles, ovals, trapezoids, and triangles. Before you get started on the drawings in this book, you might want to take a little time to practice these easy shapes. Filling up a piece of spare paper with basic shapes is a great way to practice your drawing skills — and it's a great way to loosen up, too!

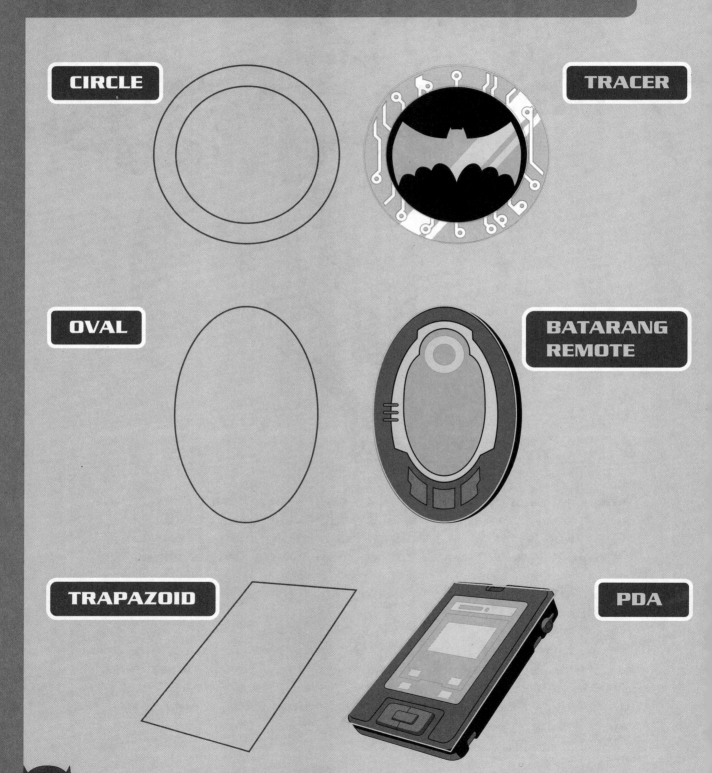

CIRCLE

TRACER

OVAL

BATARANG REMOTE

TRAPAZOID

PDA

TRIANGLES

BATGLIDER

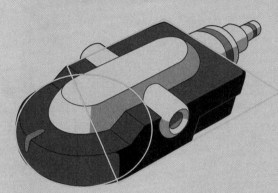

CIRCLE/TRAPEZOID

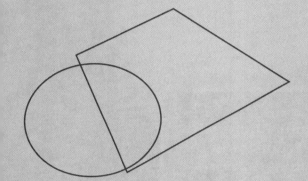

BATWAVE RECEIVER

OVALS/TRAPEZOID

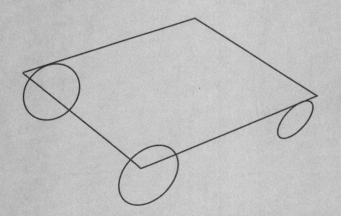

BATMOBILE

Now you're ready to tackle a more difficult task!

BRUCE WAYNE

Bruce uses his casually stylish billionaire persona to fool people into thinking he has nothing to do with the masked warrior cleaning up the nighttime streets of Gotham City.

STEP 1
Use circles and lines to make a stick figure of Bruce. Use light lines that will be easy to erase later.

STEP 2
Surround your figure with circles and trapezoids for Bruce's shoulders, arms and legs.

STEP 3
Now add basic details like Bruce's hairline and shirt.

STEP 6

Finish Bruce by adding shade lines and highlights to his suit, shoes, and shirt. Add the final touches of color and Bruce Wayne is ready to socialize with other hipsters in Gotham high society!

STEP 5

Start adding color — a medium blue for Bruce's shirt, dark gray for his suit, and black for his shoes.

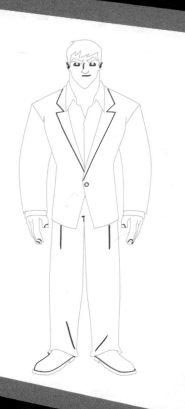

STEP 4

Okay, now add a second layer of detail, like the mouth and fingernails. Erase the light lines used to create the stick figure.

BATMAN

Driven by the tragedy of his parents' murder at the hands of a petty criminal, Batman will not rest until Gotham City is free from evildoers.

STEP 1
Start with a large, light circle for Batman's chest, and smaller ones for his head and joints.

STEP 2
Connect your basic shapes to form the outline of Batman's costume.

STEP 3
Then add the shape of Batman's cape and Utility Belt.

STEP 6
Batman is almost ready to patrol the night. Just add shade lines where you want them and — BOOM! — the Caped Crusader is ready for action.

STEP 5
Bring your drawing to life with color. Batman's famous costume is yours to create!

STEP 4
Use triangles to create the Dark Knight's flowing cape. Awesome!

CHASING A CRIMINAL

Batman stays in tip-top physical condition so he can catch crooks no matter how fast they run.

STEP 1
You can only see one leg in this drawing, so be careful!

STEP 2
Create the outline for Batman's costume.

STEP 3
Add in the detail lines for Batman's costume and mask.

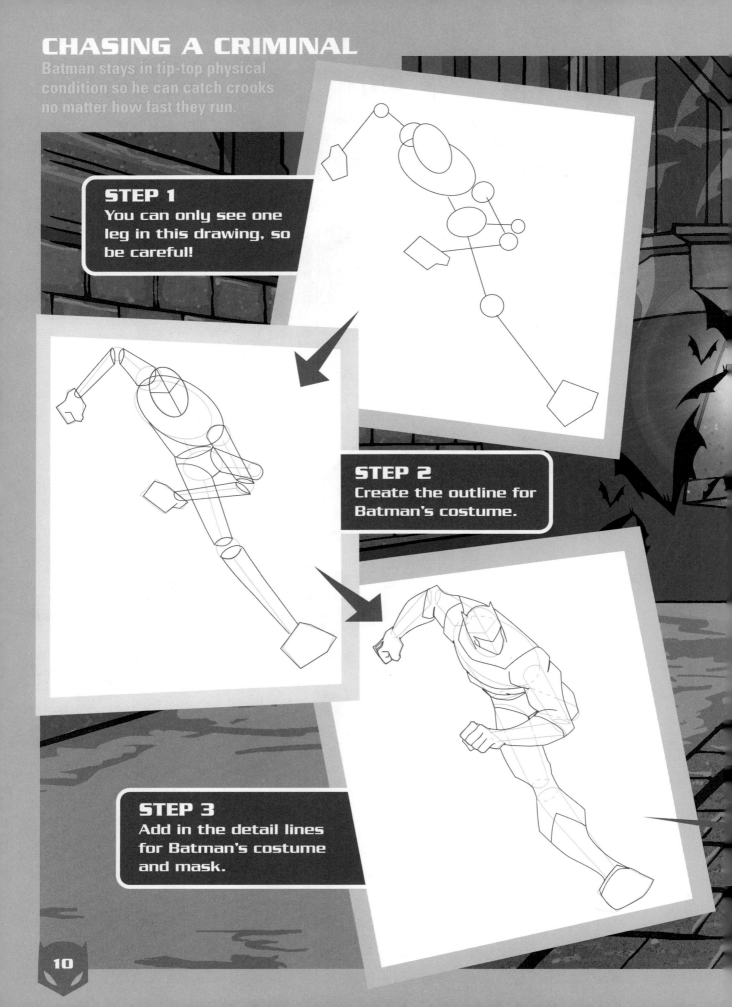

STEP 6

Apply the final layer of color, shade lines for depth, and light lines for highlights like the blue in Batman's cape.

STEP 5

Now it's time to add color to the Dark Knight — mostly blacks and grays here (except for Batman's symbol, of course).

STEP 4

Go ahead and erase the light lines you used for the outline. Then add Batman's logo, gloves, and cape. Remember, Batman is running — try to capture a sense of motion in the drawing.

11

Batman stops criminals with powerful —
and non-lethal — attacks.

STEP 1
Begin with the basic
shapes to create a
stick figure.

STEP 2
Draw the outline for the
Caped Crusader's muscles
and costume.

STEP 3
Time to add the first layer of
polish — lines for Batman's
mask, Utility Belt, and symbol
to start.

STEP 6
Put on the final layer of color and detail, and watch the cowardly criminals of Gotham City run for the shadows.

STEP 5
Add some color. In this drawing Batman is demonstrating his awesome strength. Make sure this comes through in your drawing!

STEP 4
Round off the detailing by adding light lines to show Batman's powerful arms and broad chest.

LONG ARM OF THE LAW

Batman uses a Batarang to bring crooks to justice. This elegant weapon can knock guns out of criminals' hands before they have the chance to shoot.

STEP 1
Start with the basic shapes: circles for the chest and joints. Remember to use light lines so you can erase them later.

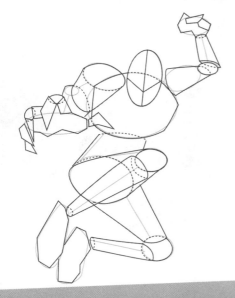

STEP 2
Draw additional shapes to fill in your drawing. Notice how one of Batman's hands is drawn larger than the other to give the illusion that it's closer. This drawing technique is called *foreshortening*.

STEP 3
Start adding detail to his costume and limbs — Batman's cape, mask, and gloves all need some attention.

STEP 6
Add a final layer of polish and Batman is prepared for anything!

STEP 5
Color in your drawing.

STEP 4
Add another layer of detail. Don't forget the Batarang in his left hand!

HIGH ABOVE GOTHAM CITY

Years of training in acrobatics and gymnastics have made Batman more agile than an Olympic athlete.

STEP 1
Because of the foreshortened angle, you will have to draw Batman's foot larger than his chest and head!

STEP 2
Use ovals and trapezoids to create the basic outline of the costume.

STEP 3
When you are ready it's time to add more of Batman's costume.

STEP 6
Now you can set the scene. After you add the final shading, draw a background like the crescent moon or the Bat Signal to make the picture your own.

STEP 5
Use color to add realism to Batman's dramatic pose.

STEP 4
Draw lines for the Batrope and triangles for the cape.

JOKER

Joker is Batman's archenemy and possibly the most dangerous villain in Gotham City. This violent clown has a flair for the dramatic . . . and is a complete madman.

STEP 1
Now it's Joker's turn! Notice the twisting, hunched position of his body. Recreate that with your stick model.

STEP 2
Create an outline to start drawing Joker's costume.

STEP 3
Add Joker's weird hair and the frayed sleeves of his shirt.

18

STEP 6
Finish your drawing by adding highlights and shading. No wonder Batman goes on high alert whenever Joker is on the loose!

STEP 5
Start adding color — green for his hair and nails, and red and yellow for his eyes.

STEP 4
Then throw on some facial details. Try to capture Joker's crazed look!

PENGUIN

Penguin is a skilled burglar who uses birds to carry out his criminal schemes. Having squandered his family fortune, Penguin now seeks to gain wealth through a life of crime.

STEP 1
Use a large circle for Penguin's wide birdlike body.

STEP 2
Connect the circles and use trapezoids and ovals to refine his shape.

STEP 3
Throw on the Penguin's top hat and the outline of his jacket.

STEP 6

Create a scene around Penguin after you add more detail and color. Remember: This is your drawing!

STEP 5

Drop on the first layer of color for this foul fowl.

STEP 4

Erase any lines you don't need, then keep fleshing out Penguin. Don't forget the tails of his tuxedo jacket!

BANE

The massive brute Bane magnifies his strength using a chemical infusion. Batman cannot hope to beat this behemoth physically — he must use his wits instead!

STEP 1
Use ovals and circles to form Bane's enormous outline.

STEP 2
Form his body with other basic shapes. Notice that Bane's arms and chest are much larger than his legs and hips.

STEP 3
Draw Bane's face and his huge muscles and fists.

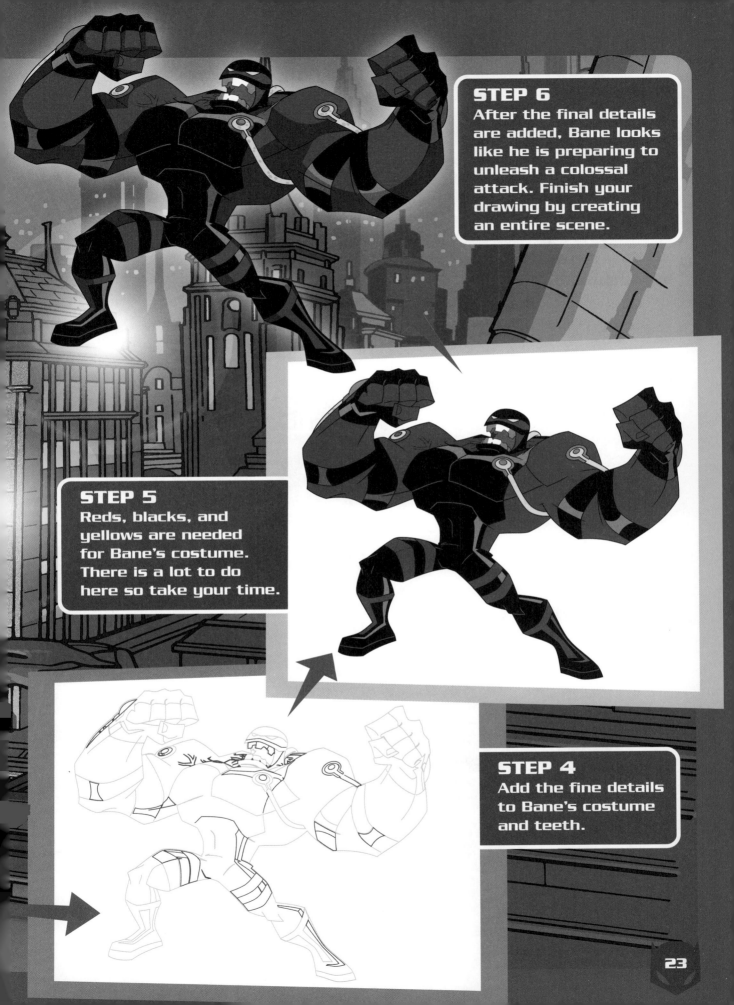

STEP 6
After the final details are added, Bane looks like he is preparing to unleash a colossal attack. Finish your drawing by creating an entire scene.

STEP 5
Reds, blacks, and yellows are needed for Bane's costume. There is a lot to do here so take your time.

STEP 4
Add the fine details to Bane's costume and teeth.

MR. FREEZE

Once a petty criminal named Victor Fries, the freakish Mr. Freeze gained his strange powers after exposure to cryogenic gases.

STEP 1
Start with a large oval for Mr. Freeze's shoulders and chest and a very small one for his head.

STEP 2
Refine the outline by shaping Mr. Freeze's shoulders and boots.

STEP 3
Time to add outlines for the icy hair and burning eyes of this villain.

STEP 6
Complete your work by adding highlights and a background — someplace cold!

STEP 5
Don't forget to color the icy vapor rolling off of Mr. Freeze's head!

STEP 4
Fill in more of Mr. Freeze's costume and face.

CATWOMAN

When socialite Selina Kyle dons her costume, she becomes Catwoman, the ultimate cat burglar . . . who just might have a little crush on Batman.

STEP 1
Catwoman has a slim, catlike figure, so use smaller ovals to start.

STEP 2
Begin creating Catwoman's costume. Don't overlook the sharp angle of her torso.

STEP 3
Draw the outline for the immense ears of Catwoman's costume, and sketch her eyes and mouth.

STEP 6
Draw in one last detail —
Catwoman's goggles —
and Selina is ready for
mischief. Create a scene
around her and let the
action begin!

STEP 5
Start bringing Catwoman
to life with color — lots
of black!

STEP 4
Get rid of the lines
you don't need, then
add Catwoman's whip.

PUTTING IT ALL TOGETHER

Use what you have learned to create cool battle scenes like this one of Batman fighting Mr. Freeze.

IMAGINE!
With some practice, the only limit
to what you can draw will be what
you can think up!

CONGRATULATIONS!
You learned to draw Batman and the villains, and you helped protect Gotham City. Great job!